ROAR!

Argh!

Yup, I've still got it.

I might not look like a beast anymore, but I can still act the part. Notice that I used the word "act"? Acting changed my life. It got me INTO trouble. It got me OUT of trouble. It even got me the girl of my dreams!

My name is Prince Elmer. If you believe the lies,
I was once a spoiled brat who refused to help
a poor old woman.

Here's the REAL story.

NO LIE, I ACTED LIKE A BEAST!

The story of BEAUTY AND THE BEAST as told by THE BEAST

by Nancy Loewen
illustrated by Cristian Bernardini

Raintree

Raintree is an imprint of Capstone Global Library Limited,
a company incorporated in England and Wales having its
registered office at 7 Pilgrim Street, London, EC4V 6LB –
Registered company number: 6695582

To contact Raintree, please email myorders@raintreepublishers.co.uk.

First published by Picture Window Books © 2013
First published in the United Kingdom in 2013
The moral rights of the proprietor have been asserted.

Editors: Laura Knowles and Jill Kalz
Art Director: Nathan Gassman
Designer: Lori Bye
Production Specialist: Jennifer Walker
Originated by Capstone Global Library Ltd
Printed and bound in China by Leo Paper Products Ltd

The illustrations in this book were created digitally.

Special thanks to our adviser, Terry Flaherty, PhD, Professor of English,
Minnesota State University, Mankato, for his expertise.

ISBN 978 1 406 26663 4 (paperback)
17 16 15 14 13
10 9 8 7 6 5 4 3 2 1

British Library Cataloguing in Publication Data
A full catalogue record for this book is available from the British Library.

As a young prince, I was shy – so shy that I wouldn't even answer the phone. And if a pretty girl came around, forget it!

One day I read a notice in the newspaper.

THEATRE AUDITIONS FOR

"THE THREE BILLY GOATS GRUFF"

I decided then and there that I was done with being shy. I was going to find my voice – as an actor!

Of course I wanted the best part in the play: the evil troll who lives under the bridge. So I practiced. And practiced.

I barked and hissed.

I growled as I
brushed my teeth.

I slashed at
the air with
my fork.

On audition night, my head was so full of troll thoughts that at first I didn't notice the tug on my sleeve. It was a poor old woman asking for food.

"NO!" I roared. "I WON'T HELP YOU. GO AWAY!"

Then I remembered that I wasn't actually a troll. "Oh! I'm so sorry, I was just –"

But it was too late. Before my eyes, the old woman became an evil fairy. "Fool!" she cried. "You act like a beast. You shall BE a beast!"

"But you don't understand –"

"There is only one way to break this spell," the evil fairy said. "A woman must fall in love with you, in spite of your looks!" She sniggered. "Like that's going to happen."

I must've fainted, because the next thing I knew,
I was in a strange castle. In the woods. Alone.

That was the worst time of my life. I was
hideous. Oh, sure, I had all sorts of fine things.
But I had no one to talk to.

To pass the time, I kept up my acting studies. In the garden I put on one-man shows for the birds and the butterflies.

Then came the stormy night that changed everything. A lost traveller took shelter in my castle. I remained hidden, but I made sure he had everything he needed. It felt awfully nice to have company.

The next morning, as he was leaving, he took a rose from the garden. That gave me an idea. Maybe I could trick him into coming back.

I'm not proud of what I did next, but it worked!

"IS THAT HOW YOU REWARD MY KINDNESS?" I roared.
"YOU WILL PAY WITH YOUR LIFE!"

13

The man begged to say goodbye to his family.
He promised to return.

And he did – with his daughter named Beauty.
Beauty had vowed to take her father's place.
She felt responsible because she was the one
who'd asked for a rose.

For me, it was love at first sight. For
her – not so much. Who could blame
her? I had fur growing out of my
nostrils. And I smelled like a barn.

I went back to my shy ways, hiding behind drapes and ducking into wardrobes. After a few days passed, Beauty worked out that I was more of a teddy bear than a beast. Imagine my delight when SHE started talking to ME.

We had a lot in common – including a love of good theatre. I didn't have to do one-man shows anymore. I had a co-star! The more Beauty and I acted together, the more she got to know the real me.

One day, Beauty asked to leave the castle.
She wanted to visit her family.

"OK, but you'd better come back. I'll die without
you," I joked. And then my voice became serious.
"Really. If you leave me, I'll die."

Yes, it was a bit over the top. What can I say?
I'm an actor.

And with that,
she left.

When Beauty returned, she found me lying on the
ground next to the rose bush. I tried not to breathe.

"Beast?" Beauty cried out. "Oh, no!"

Her tears poured onto my fur, but I didn't move.

"Oh, Beast, you're the ugliest creature I've ever seen.
But – I can't help it, I love you! I do!"

21

And just like that, the spell was broken.
I got my Happily Ever After.

I was a prince again.

I married Beauty.

And together we've opened the Prince
Elmer School of Beastly Good Acting.

You should take a class. It might
change your life!

Think about it

Fairy tales have been around a long time, and they often have many different versions. What version of *Beauty and the Beast* do you know best? How is it different from this one? How is it the same?

How do you think this story would be different if it was told from another character's point of view? How about Beauty? Beauty's father?

Imagine living in a world in which fairies, witches, or other magical beings could appear at any moment. How would that affect your actions?

Prince Elmer was "in character" when he was rude to the old woman (who was actually an evil fairy). Have you ever been so lost in thought that you did something you really felt bad about? Even if Prince Elmer had been rude on purpose, do you think he would have deserved such punishment? Why or why not?

⤳⤳❦⤳⤳

Glossary

character person, animal, or creature in a story
point of view way of looking at something
version particular form of something

23

Find out more

Books

Mixed Up Fairy Tales, Hilary Robinson, illustrated by Nick Sharratt (Hodder, 2005).

The Orchard Book of Hans Christian Andersen's Fairy Tales, Martin Waddell (Orchard, 2010).

Usborne Illustrated Grimm's Fairy Tales, Ruth Brockelhurst and Gillian Doherty (Usborne, 2012).

Website

storynory.com/archives/fairy-tales
Visit this website to listen to some of the best-loved fairy tales.

Other books in the series

Believe Me, Goldilocks Rocks!   978 1 406 24309 3
Honestly, Red Riding Hood Was Rotten!   978 1 406 24310 9
Seriously, Cinderella Is So Annoying!   978 1 406 24311 6
Seriously, Snow White was So Forgetful!   978 1 406 26664 1
Trust Me, Jack's Beanstalk Stinks!   978 1 406 24312 3